Super Duck to the Rescue

by Liza Charlesworth

ISBN: 978-1-338-89046-4

Designer: Cynthia Ng; Illustrated by John Lund

Copyright © 2023 by Liza Charlesworth. All rights reserved. Published by Scholastic Inc.

1 2 3 4 5 6 7 8 9 10   68   31 30 29 28 27 26 25 24 23 22

Printed in Jiaxing, China. First printing, January 2023.

Meet Super Duck.
Super Duck is brave in his dreams.
He always saves the day.
But guess what?

Super Duck is NOT brave in real life.
In fact, he is afraid of EVERYTHING.
Super Duck is afraid to walk in the garden.
"Quack, quack!" he cries.
"That garden looks VERY scary!"

Super Duck is afraid to jump
in the pond and swim.
"Quack, quack!" he cries.
"That pond looks VERY scary!"

Super Duck is afraid to visit his pals
in the big red barn.
"Quack, quack!" he cries.
"That barn looks VERY scary!"

Super Duck is afraid to flap
his feathered wings and fly.
In fact, he's never EVEN tried.
"Quack, quack!" he cries.
"Being up high looks VERY, VERY scary!"

Super Duck's friend, Kitty,
always likes to tease him.
"HELP ME, HELP ME!" he yells.
"Oh, I forgot: You can't help me
because you're afraid of EVERYTHING."
Kitty makes Super Duck feel sad.

But Kitty isn't done yet.
"Watch what I can do!" he brags
as he climbs higher and higher in the tree.
"Quack, quack!" cries Super Duck.
"I wish I was brave like Kitty."
This makes Super Duck feel even sadder...

...until he hears a loud *C-R-A-C-K!*
"HELP ME, HELP ME!" yells Kitty
from the top of the tree.
"Very funny," responds Super Duck.
"I am not going to fall for that one."

"NO REALLY, REALLY!" yells Kitty.
"The branch I was standing on just broke."
So Super Duck looks up and sees Kitty
hanging onto the tree by his claws.
Guess what? Kitty is NOT kidding!

Super Duck needs to help Kitty right away.
And this time, he doesn't have
one second to be afraid.
"Quack, quack!" he cries.
"Super Duck to the rescue!"

Super Duck flaps his wings.
Flap, flap, flap!

Super Duck flies up, up, up
to the tippy top of the tree.

Super Duck cries, "Quack, quack!
Jump on my back!"

Kitty jumps on Super Duck's back.
Flap, flap, flap!

Flap, flap, flap!
Super Duck flies Kitty
back down to the ground.
Kitty is scared and shaking,
but he is safe and sound.

"You are my hero!" cries Kitty.
"I'm sorry I said you were afraid.
I was wrong: You are super brave!"
Then he adds, "And by the way,
did you notice that you CAN fly?"

Flap, flap, flap!
This time, Kitty IS telling the truth.
Super Duck feels super proud of himself.
And from now on, he can save the day
in his dreams…and in real life, too!